S0-AHS-206

ROOOOAAAAARRRR

WE HEAR IT
BEFORE WE
SEE IT—

UP AND DOWN
THE SIDEWALK,
PEOPLE FREEZE.

I'VE NEVER
SEEN A PLANE
FLY SO LOW.

THE BRIGHT
BLUE SKY . . .

FILLS WITH FIRE
AND SMOKE . . .

SO MUCH
SMOKE.

I SURVIVED

THE ATTACKS OF SEPTEMBER 11, 2001

BASED ON THE NOVEL IN THE *NEW YORK TIMES*
BESTSELLING SERIES BY LAUREN TARSHIS

ADAPTED BY GEORGIA BALL
WITH ART BY COREY EGBERT
COLORS BY CHI NGO

graphix

AN IMPRINT OF

📖 SCHOLASTIC

About two weeks earlier . . .
WEDNESDAY, AUGUST 29

Port Jackson, New York
10:00 a.m.

PRACTICE IS BRUTAL, AS USUAL.

IT'S 95 DEGREES, AND I'M COVERED IN SWEAT.

HUT!

IT'S AN IMPOSSIBLE CATCH . . .

MY FAVORITE KIND.

UMPH

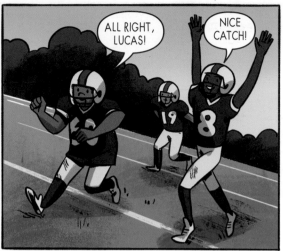

ALL RIGHT, LUCAS!

NICE CATCH!

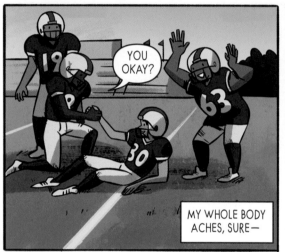

YOU OKAY?

MY WHOLE BODY ACHES, SURE—

—BUT THIS IS WHERE I BELONG.

IT'S JUST LIKE UNCLE BENNY ALWAYS SAYS . . .

YOU HAVE TO BELIEVE YOU'RE GOING TO CATCH THE BALL.

YOU HAVE TO FEEL IT IN YOUR HEART.

I BLACK OUT.

HOME? THIS IS YOUR FIRST PRACTICE! YOU DON'T WANT TO GO HOME!

YES, I DID!

NO, YOU DON'T!

LUCAS, YOU'VE TRAINED SO HARD. ALL THOSE AFTERNOONS TOSSING THE BALL AROUND WITH ME!

YOU DON'T WANT TO KEEP ALL THAT HARD WORK TO YOURSELF! YOU WANT TO GO OUT THERE—

—AND SHOW THEM WHAT YOU CAN DO.

AND FROM THAT DAY ON, I FELT LIKE I'D FOUND MY PLACE.

I'M PROUD OF YOU, KID.

THANKS, UNCLE BENNY.

EVEN NOW, IT'S NOT SO MUCH ABOUT THE GAME . . .

I LOVE BEING ON A TEAM WITH THE OTHER GUYS.

WE WATCH EACH OTHER'S BACKS.

WIN OR LOSE . . .

PORT JACKSON JAGUARS STICK TOGETHER.

I'M FINE.

LOOKS LIKE YOU HAVE ANOTHER CONCUSSION.

SURE, IT'S WORSE THAN THE CONCUSSION I GOT DURING PLAYOFFS LAST SEASON —

— AND THE ONE I GOT THE SUMMER AFTER FOURTH GRADE.

BUT I'LL GET BETTER IF I TAKE IT EASY.

WHAT REALLY KILLS ME IS KNOWING I'LL BE OFF THE FIELD FOR TWELVE DAYS.

I ALREADY MISS THE GUYS.

WHEN I CALLED UNCLE BENNY EARLIER, HE SAID TO KEEP MY CHIN UP.

UNCLE BENNY'S ALWAYS LIKE THAT— IN YOUR CORNER.

UNCLE BENNY ISN'T ACTUALLY MY UNCLE. HE'S MY DAD'S BEST FRIEND FROM LADDER 177, THE FIREHOUSE WHERE THEY WORK IN NEW YORK CITY.

DAD SAYS UNCLE BENNY'S LIKE THE FIREHOUSE CHEERLEADER—

HIS FIRST REAL FIRE. YOU SHOULD HAVE SEEN HIM.

IT WAS JUST A LITTLE ONE IN A GARBAGE CAN.

EVERYBODY'S GOT TO START SOMEWHERE, CORY. YOU MIGHT BE STARTING AT THE BOTTOM—

—BUT YOU'RE GOING TO LOVE EVERY MINUTE OF THIS JOB, I PROMISE YOU.

—A CHEERLEADER WITH A SHAMROCK TATTOO.

26

I GOT TO KNOW UNCLE BENNY WHEN DAD WAS HURT IN A WAREHOUSE FIRE.

DAD WAS IN THE HOSPITAL BURN CENTER FOR TWO MONTHS.

UNCLE BENNY PRACTICALLY MOVED IN WITH US UNTIL DAD WAS BETTER.

I USED TO WAKE UP AND FIND HIM READING THE SPORTS PAGES IN THE NEWSPAPER.

DAD AND I WERE TOO BUSY FOR SPORTS.

BEFORE DAD GOT HURT, WE SPENT EVERY WEEKEND IN THE BASEMENT WORKSHOP.

WE WERE BUILDING A MODEL OF THE LADDER 177 TRUCK—

—THE SEAGRAVE 75.

UNCLE BENNY ISN'T INTERESTED IN TRUCK MODELS.

HE LOVES FOOTBALL.

SOON ENOUGH, I WAS WATCHING ESPN AND *MONDAY NIGHT FOOTBALL* RIGHT ALONG WITH HIM.

WE CHEERED FOR HIS FAVORITE TEAMS—

—AND BOOED THE PLAYERS UNCLE BENNY HATED.

HE TOLD ME ALL ABOUT HIS TIME PLAYING FOR HIS COLLEGE FOOTBALL TEAM.

THEN HE BOUGHT ME A FOOTBALL . . .

AND WE SPENT HOURS IN THE BACKYARD WHILE I LEARNED HOW TO THROW AND CATCH.

I OWE FOOTBALL TO UNCLE BENNY.

HE'LL BE LOOKING FORWARD TO ME GETTING BACK INTO THE GAME AS MUCH AS I AM.

HEY, BUDDY. FEELING OKAY?

HI, DAD. I'M GOOD.

NEED ANYTHING?

NOPE, I'M GOOD.

I STAY VERY STILL.

MAYBE HE'LL STICK AROUND AND TALK, LIKE HE USED TO.

31

DAD USED TO PLOP DOWN NEXT TO ME EVERY NIGHT TO CHAT AND PLAN OUR NEXT ADVENTURE.

SOMETIMES WE'D WAIT FOR MOM TO FALL ASLEEP SO WE COULD SNEAK DOWN TO THE BASEMENT.

WE WERE A TEAM—

— UNTIL THE WAREHOUSE FIRE.

I KNEW DAD'S JOB WAS DANGEROUS.

SOMETIMES DAD TAKES ME TO THE FIREHOUSE ON HIS DAYS OFF.

I LIKE HELPING OUT WITH THE CHORES.

BUT WHAT I LOVE MOST IS HEARING THE GUYS TALK ABOUT THE FIRES THEY'VE FOUGHT.

TELL ME AGAIN ABOUT THE FIRE ON 36TH STREET, GEORGIE!

RIGHT, THAT ONE . . .

SO THERE I WAS ON THE FIRE ESCAPE . . .

THE METAL IS BURNING LIKE AN OVEN.

FIREFIGHTERS LIKE GEORGIE AND DAD AND UNCLE BENNY RUN INTO BUILDINGS FILLED WITH BLAZING ORANGE FLAMES—

CRASH

— AND CHOKING BLACK SMOKE.

THEY RIP OUT WALLS AND BASH THROUGH DOORS.

THEY DANGLE FROM ROPES HIGH UP IN THE AIR.

TO ME . . .

BUT IT WASN'T UNTIL THE WAREHOUSE FIRE THAT I REALLY UNDERSTOOD WHAT A FIRE COULD DO TO A PERSON—

DING DONG

— EVEN TO SUPERHEROES LIKE DAD.

THE MEMORY IS SO SHARP.

CHIEF AND UNCLE BENNY, OUTSIDE OUR FRONT DOOR.

THEY REEKED OF SMOKE.

THAT WAS THREE YEARS AGO.

DAD NEVER TALKS ABOUT WHAT HAPPENED THAT NIGHT.

ALL I KNOW IS THAT FOUR FIREFIGHTERS DIED IN THE EXPLOSION THAT BURNED HIM.

EVEN NOW, THE SCARS ON HIS ARM ARE RED AND LUMPY—

— LIKE RAW HAMBURGER MEAT.

BUT THE BURNS AREN'T THE WORST THING THE FIRE DID TO DAD.

I STOPPED ASKING WHEN WE'LL GET BACK TO THE SEAGRAVE.

IT'S COLLECTING DUST, HALF-FINISHED.

WHENEVER THE MEMORIES OF THAT NIGHT COME BACK—

— OR I WORRY THAT DAD WILL NEVER BE HIMSELF AGAIN—

CLICK

I CLOSE MY EYES—

—AND I'M BACK ON THE FIELD.

80

I CAN'T WAIT FOR TOMORROW!

FINALLY, I CAN GET BACK IN THE GAME . . .

OKAY, OKAY. I JUST WANT THE NEW DOCTOR TO CHECK YOU OUT FIRST.

I HEAR HE'S THE BEST.

I'M FINE, CAN'T YOU TELL?

HA-HA . . . VERY IMPRESSIVE!

"BUT DR. BARRETT IS A LEADING SPECIALIST . . ."

"WE'RE LUCKY HE COULD FIT YOU IN."

HI, LUCAS, I'M DR. BARRETT.

LET'S TAKE A LOOK AT YOU.

HE LOOKS MORE LIKE A LINEBACKER THAN A DOCTOR.

NOW, WALK ACROSS THE ROOM FOR ME. ONE FOOT IN FRONT OF THE OTHER.

FINE! GOOD . . .

ALL OF THOSE MEN UP THERE ARE DEAD, LUCAS.

THEY DIED YOUNG BECAUSE OF THEIR CONCUSSIONS.

THEY DONATED THEIR BRAINS TO OUR LAB SO WE COULD STUDY THEM.

THEY ALL HAD THE SAME KIND OF BRAIN DISEASE YOU USUALLY SEE IN PEOPLE IN THEIR EIGHTIES.

WE USED TO THINK CONCUSSIONS WERE LIKE SPRAINED ANKLES . . .

YOU GET DINGED, YOU LET IT HEAL, YOU'RE GOOD TO GO.

BUT NOW WE KNOW THAT TOO MANY CONCUSSIONS CAN ACTUALLY CHANGE THE BRAIN.

HOW MANY CONCUSSIONS IS TOO MANY?

I HOLD MY BREATH.

I DON'T THINK I WANT TO HEAR THE ANSWER.

I WOULD SAY THAT IN AN ELEVEN-YEAR-OLD BOY . . .

THREE CONCUSSIONS IN TWO YEARS IS TOO MANY.

THE ROOM GOES QUIET.

I CAN FEEL THE EYES OF THOSE FOOTBALL PLAYERS LOOKING DOWN ON ME.

I CAN STAY ON THE BENCH AT PRACTICE FOR ANOTHER WEEK!

≋SIGH≋

I'M SORRY, LUCAS . . .

I'M SUGGESTING THAT YOU NEVER PLAY FOOTBALL AGAIN.

I ARGUE AND BEG ALL NIGHT.

THE DOCTOR IS WRONG, HE *HAS* TO BE!

LUCAS . . .

WHAT ABOUT LEVON AMES? HE'S MORE THAN FORTY AND HE'S STILL PLAYING!

IT'S NOT ABOUT OTHER PLAYERS. THIS IS ABOUT YOU.

WE WANT YOU TO BE SAFE.

BUT WATCHING ALL OF THE OTHER GUYS PLAY WITHOUT ME . . .

IT'LL BE TORTURE!

I'LL SIT OUT FOR TWO MORE WEEKS . . .

LUCAS . . .

NO, *THREE!*

JUST . . .

PLEASE DON'T MAKE ME QUIT.

LUCAS . . .

FOOTBALL IS A GAME.

I KNOW YOU LOVE IT.

BUT IT'S JUST A GAME.

A GAME.

I KNOW THAT.

OF COURSE I KNOW THAT.

BUT THAT *GAME* IS THE MOST IMPORTANT THING IN MY WHOLE LIFE.

WHAT AM I GOING TO DO WITHOUT MY TEAM?

THERE HAS TO BE SOMETHING I CAN DO . . .

≡GASP!≡

UNCLE BENNY!

I'VE GOT TO SEE UNCLE BENNY BEFORE MOM AND DAD TALK TO COACH—

—BEFORE IT'S TOO LATE.

The next morning . . .

I'D BETTER GET GOING.

I'M TEACHING A CLASS AT THE ROCK TODAY.

THE ROCK IS A FIREFIGHTER TRAINING SCHOOL ON RANDALL'S ISLAND.

MOM DROPS ME OFF AT THE BUS STOP.

HAVE A GOOD DAY!

LOVE YOU . . .

TIME TO GO.

I UNLOCKED OUR GARAGE DOOR THIS MORNING.

CREEAAKK

I TAKE OFF—

— STRAIGHT FOR THE TRAIN STATION.

I CATCH THE 7:17 TRAIN WITH ONE MINUTE TO SPARE.

I KNOW THIS IS WRONG.

SKIPPING SCHOOL . . .

SNEAKING INTO THE CITY . . .

LYING TO MOM AND DAD.

BUT NONE OF THAT MATTERS RIGHT NOW.

I HAVE TO SEE UNCLE BENNY.

SOMEHOW . . .

HE'LL MAKE THIS RIGHT.

I'VE MADE THIS TRIP INTO THE CITY WITH DAD SO MANY TIMES, I KNOW IT BY HEART.

SCREEE...

TAKE THE TRAIN TO PENN STATION . . .

TAKE THE SUBWAY DOWNTOWN TO CANAL STREET.

Ⓐ Downtown & Bklyn

WHEN I GET OUT OF THE SUBWAY, I SEE MY LANDMARK—

—THE TWIN TOWERS OF THE WORLD TRADE CENTER.

THE WORLD TRADE CENTER IS NINE BLOCKS SOUTH OF THE FIRE STATION.

I WALK TOWARD THE FIRE STATION—

— USING THE TOWERS AS MY GUIDE.

I REMEMBER THE LAST TIME I VISITED THE WORLD TRADE CENTER WITH DAD . . .

IT WAS RIGHT BEFORE THE WAREHOUSE FIRE.

DO THE PEOPLE REALLY LOOK LIKE ANTS?

IT'S SO HIGH AT THE TOP YOU CAN'T EVEN *SEE* ANY PEOPLE!

I'M SORRY, BUT YOU CAN'T GO UP THERE.

THE OBSERVATION DECK ISN'T OPEN YET.

OH, WAIT . . . ARE YOU WITH THE NEW YORK CITY FIRE DEPARTMENT?

SURE AM. LADDER 177.

YOU TWO GO ON AHEAD.

FEELS LIKE A LONG TIME AGO.

WHEN I GET TO THE FIREHOUSE, THE GARAGE DOOR IS OPEN.

LADDER 177

AND RIGHT NEXT TO THE SEAGRAVE—

—IS UNCLE BENNY.

IT'S OKAY, YOU CAN COME CLOSER.

KIDS ARE ALWAYS STOPPING BY TO GET A PEEK AT THE TRUCK—

LUCAS!

HOW'S IT GOING?

FIREFIGHTERS FROM THE LAST SHIFT ARE SAYING GOODBYE.

THE MORNING MEN AND WOMEN ARE JUST GETTING SETTLED.

LUCAS!

HEY, MARK!

YOU'RE GROWING LIKE A WEED.

FDNY

THAT'S WHAT PEOPLE KEEP TELLING ME.

WHERE YOU BEEN LATELY, LUCAS?

I'VE MISSED MY ASSISTANT COOK.

FDNY

AND I'VE MISSED GEORGIE'S FAMOUS TOMATO SAUCE!

HIS EIGHT-YEAR-OLD TWINS ARE FOOTBALL FANATICS.

MARK COACHES THEIR TEAM.

LAST SEASON THEY CAME TO ONE OF MY GAMES.

AWESOME TOUCHDOWN, DERRICK!

THANKS!

LUCAS?

OH, HEY! YOU'RE JASON, RIGHT?

YEAH— GOOD GUESS! AND THIS IS JAMES.

CAN WE HAVE YOUR AUTOGRAPH?

SURE, MAN. ANYTIME.

66

IT'S BECAUSE OF MY CONCUSSIONS.

YEAH...

I'VE BEEN WORRIED ABOUT YOU, KIDDO.

YOU'VE GOT A DARNED GOOD BRAIN.

I DON'T WANT YOU TO END UP LIKE POOR STAN WALSH.

THEN IT HITS ME—

— UNCLE BENNY MUST HAVE ASKED MOM TO TAKE ME TO DR. BARRETT! STAN WALSH'S DOCTOR.

I CAME ALL THIS WAY SO UNCLE BENNY WOULD HELP ME—

— BUT *HE'S* THE REASON I HAVE TO QUIT!

69

IT FEELS LIKE UNCLE BENNY IS TRYING TO KEEP ME PINNED TO THE GROUND—

—SO I DON'T FLY AWAY.

YOU'LL FIND SOMETHING ELSE.

SOMETHING ELSE?

WHAT ELSE DO I HAVE?

ROOOAAAAARRRR

CALL DISPATCH...

A PLANE JUST CRASHED INTO THE WORLD TRADE CENTER!

THIS IS A 10-60...

A 10-60?

THAT'S RIGHT, I SAID A 10-60!

THAT'S THE WORST KIND OF ALARM!

THEN I REALIZE...

THERE MUST BE THOUSANDS OF PEOPLE TRAPPED IN THAT TOWER.

AND NO MATTER HOW DANGEROUS IT MIGHT BE—

—PEOPLE LIKE DAD AND UNCLE BENNY ARE GOING TO TRY TO SAVE THEM.

IT CAN TAKE TWO MINUTES FOR A FIREFIGHTER TO WALK UP ONE FLIGHT OF STAIRS.

YOU GOT A FIRE AT THE TOP OF A HIGH-RISE? ADD IT UP.

THE FIRE IS NEAR THE TOP OF THE WORLD TRADE CENTER— MAYBE THE EIGHTIETH OR NINETIETH FLOOR.

IT COULD BE *TWO HOURS* BEFORE THE FIREFIGHTERS GET THERE!

CAN THE PEOPLE ON THOSE FLOORS WAIT THAT LONG FOR HELP?!

YOUR DAD IS HEADING TO THE SCENE!

I TOLD HIM YOU'D STAY HERE AND WAIT FOR HIM.

YOU SIT TIGHT, OKAY?

TAKE CARE OF THINGS FOR US, BUDDY!

ARRRRRRRRRRRRRR

THE GARAGE DOOR SHUTS . . .

I'M ALONE.

PLEASE PICK UP, MOM . . .

LEAVE YOUR MESSAGE AFTER THE BEEP . . .

BEEEP

MOM . . . I'M AT THE FIREHOUSE . . .

I KNOW— I KNOW I'M NOT SUPPOSED TO BE HERE . . .

BUT I'M FINE! PLEASE CALL ME . . .

CLICK

MY MIND IS SPINNING

"WE'LL DO WHAT WE ALWAYS DO . . ."

FIGHT FIRES.

SAVE LIVES.

THE NEW YORK CITY FIRE DEPARTMENT IS ONE OF THE BIGGEST FIRE DEPARTMENTS IN THE WORLD.

THEY'RE THE BEST.

THEY'LL DO WHAT THEY ALWAYS DO.

IT'S LIKE WHAT DAD SAID ONCE . . .

WHAT DO YOU LIKE MOST ABOUT BEING A FIREMAN?

EVERYONE'S GOT A JOB TO DO.

IF YOU DON'T WORK TOGETHER, YOU DON'T PUT OUT THE FIRE.

JUST A FEW MINUTES AGO, A PLANE CRASHED INTO TOWER ONE AT NEW YORK'S FAMED WORLD TRADE CENTER.

WE HAVE NO OFFICIAL INFORMATION ABOUT WHAT KIND OF PLANE IT WAS . . .

"BUT WITNESSES REPORT IT WAS A COMMERCIAL JET.

"THE TOWERS WERE COMPLETED IN 1973 . . .

"AT 110 FLOORS EACH, THEY WERE ONCE THE TALLEST BUILDINGS IN THE WORLD."

THERE ARE NOW HUNDREDS OF FIREFIGHTERS ON THE SCENE.

WE HAVE REPORTS THAT FIREFIGHTERS HAVE ENTERED THE BUILDING AND ARE GOING UP THE STAIRS TO REACH PEOPLE WHO MIGHT NEED THEIR ASSISTANCE.

"IT'S A JAW-DROPPING SIGHT."

WHITE DOTS ARE FLOATING IN THE SMOKE.

PAPER.

MILLIONS OF PIECES OF PAPER . . .

SWEPT OUT THROUGH THE HOLE IN THE BUILDING.

THE WORLD TRADE CENTER TOWERS TOOK MORE THAN THREE YEARS TO BUILD.

THEY CAN WITHSTAND WINDS OF 140 OR MORE PER HOUR.

APPROXIMATELY FIFTY THOUSAND PEOPLE WORK IN THE TOWERS EVERY DAY.

SHE SOUNDS SO CALM.

LIKE A HISTORY TEACHER.

"THE NORTH TOWER STANDS AT 1,368 FEET IN THE AIR, WHILE THE SOUTH TOWER—

"OH MY GOODNESS . . . WHAT WAS *THAT*?"

MY HEART IS POUNDING.

IT'S HARD TO BREATHE.

"OH, THAT LOOKED . . .

"WHAT DID WE JUST SEE?"

LADIES AND GENTLEMEN . . .

MOM . . .

TAP TAP
TAP
TAP
TAP

ALL CIRCUITS ARE BUSY . . .

DAD . . .

TAP
TAP
TAP
TAP

EEEP
EEEP
EEEP

≡CRACKLE≡ RECALL, RECALL . . .

ALL PERSONNEL, ON AND OFF DUTY, ARE TO REPORT.

TAP
TAP
TAP
TAP

I REPEAT. THIS IS A RECALL OF ALL PERSONNEL . . .

THERE ARE ELEVEN THOUSAND FIREFIGHTERS IN THE NYC FIRE DEPARTMENT . . .

THEY NEED EVERY SINGLE ONE.

CLICK

I CAN'T BE ALONE WATCHING THE WORLD FALL APART ON TV.

I NEED TO FIND DAD AND UNCLE BENNY.

WAAHOOOWAAAAHOOOWAAHOOWA

HONNNK HONNK

HONNK HONNNK

AAAIIIEEEEEE

SOB

ALL THE SOUNDS CRASH TOGETHER INTO ONE TERRIBLE SONG.

I KNOW I'M NOT THINKING CLEARLY RIGHT NOW.

I DON'T KNOW IF I CAN GET CLOSE—

—OR IF IT'S EVEN SAFE TO TRY.

WHAT DID THAT WOMAN ON TV SAY?

SOME KIND OF ATTACK . . .

DID SHE MEAN THOSE PLANES HIT THE TOWERS ON *PURPOSE*?

SOME KIND OF ATTACK . . .

IT'S THE ONLY THING THAT MAKES SENSE.

BUT WHO COULD BE INSANE ENOUGH—

—*EVIL* ENOUGH—

—TO FLY PLANES INTO BUILDINGS?

SOME PEOPLE ARE RUNNING.

MOST PEOPLE LOOK LIKE THEY'RE IN SHOCK . . .

JUST STANDING AROUND, DAZED.

VESEY AND WEST STREETS . . .

THAT'S WHERE THE FIREFIGHTERS ARE GATHERING.

IF DAD MADE IT HERE FROM RANDALL'S ISLAND, THAT'S WHERE I'LL FIND HIM.

MORE AND MORE PEOPLE ARE COMING FROM THE DIRECTION OF THE TOWERS.

SOME OF THEM ARE SOAKED IN SWEAT.

BUT IT'S THE LOOKS ON THEIR FACES THAT TELL ME WHERE THEY CAME FROM—

—INSIDE THE TOWERS.

THERE ARE DOZENS OF THEM.

NO ONE IS CARRYING A PURSE OR BRIEFCASE.

SOME OF THE WOMEN ARE BAREFOOT.

I KNOW WHY.

CLICK
CLICK
CLICK
CLICK

SOMETIMES PEOPLE WHO SURVIVE FIRES ESCAPE WITH SECONDS TO SPARE.

IF THEY HAD STOPPED FOR ANYTHING—

—THEY WOULDN'T HAVE MADE IT.

EVERYONE, PLEASE LEAVE THIS AREA!

IT'S NOT SAFE...

PLEASE LEAVE THIS AREA AND GO NORTH.

NOBODY TRIES TO STOP ME.

I FEEL INVISIBLE.

UNTIL . . .

HEY!

WHERE ARE YOU GOING? ARE YOU LOST?

I NEED TO FIND—

LUCAS!

I LEFT RANDALL'S ISLAND AND DROVE BACK HERE AS SOON AS THE FIRST PLANE HIT.

I WAS HEADED FOR THE SCENE, BUT I GOT THE MESSAGE YOU WERE AT THE FIREHOUSE—

—SO I WENT THERE FIRST.

CHIEF SAID YOU'D BE WAITING FOR ME.

I'M SORRY . . . I JUST COULDN'T STAY . . .

I . . .

IT'S OKAY. IT DOESN'T MATTER.

I REALIZE NOTHING THAT HAPPENED BEFORE THIS MORNING MATTERS ANYMORE.

NOT NOW . . .

MAYBE NOT EVER AGAIN.

WE NEED TO FIND THE TEAM.

I'LL GET MY GEAR FROM THE TRUCK, AND THEN I'M GOING TO FIND SOMEONE TO TAKE YOU BACK TO THE FIREHOUSE.

THEY'RE NOT GOING TO BE ABLE TO PUT THE FIRES OUT.

THIS IS A RESCUE OPERATION NOW.

WE JUST WANT TO GET ALL THE PEOPLE OUT.

CRACKLE CRACKLE

I CAN HEAR MUFFLED VOICES MIXED WITH THE STATIC.

CLICK CLICK CLICK

THE RADIOS ARE OVERLOADED.

NOBODY CAN TALK TO ANYONE NOW. PEOPLE ARE SHUT OFF.

WE CAN'T GET THROUGH TO THE GUYS IN THE TOWERS.

LUCKY.

NOTHING ABOUT THIS IS *LUCKY.*

I TRY TO KEEP MY EYES STRAIGHT AHEAD.

CAN YOU HELP ME? MY HEART . . .

I CAME DOWN THE STAIRS . . . MY FRIENDS . . .

I DON'T KNOW WHERE THEY ARE . . .

THERE WAS SO MUCH SMOKE . . .

OKAY! IT'S OKAY.

I CAN TELL DAD DOESN'T WANT TO STOP HERE.

HE WANTS TO FIND HIS CREW.

DON'T WORRY.

WE'RE GOING TO GET YOU WHAT YOU NEED.

GO TELL THE PARAMEDICS WE NEED HELP.

THERE'S A WOMAN WHO MIGHT HAVE SOMETHING WRONG WITH HER HEART.

WE'LL BE THERE AS SOON AS WE CAN.

WHAT'S YOUR NAME?

JILLIAN.

WHERE DO YOU LIVE?

WESTPORT, CONNECTICUT.

I'VE BEEN THERE. NICE PLACE! YOU GOT FAMILY THERE?

MY DAUGHTER. HER HUSBAND . . .

I'M A NEW YORK CITY FIREMAN, AND THIS IS MY SON HERE.

WE'LL MAKE SURE YOU'RE TAKEN CARE OF.

DAD KEEPS TRYING TO CALM THIS PERSON HE'S NEVER EVEN MET—

—AND PROBABLY WON'T EVER SEE AGAIN.

MA'AM?
WE'RE HERE
TO HELP.

PARAMEDIC

PARAMED

THE PARAMEDICS
TAKE JILLIAN AWAY
ON A STRETCHER—

NY

—AND WE CAN GET BACK
TO FINDING THE CREW.

LET'S GO.

RUMBLE RUMBLE RUMBLE RUMBLE

WAIT . . .

IT'S THE LOUDEST SOUND I'VE EVER HEARD.

LOUDER THAN A HUNDRED FREIGHT TRAINS.

LUCAS!

≈PTOO≈

DAD! I'M—
HERE . . .

COUGH
COUGH

HACK

IS ANYBODY
HURT?

COUGH

DUST IS EVERYWHERE.

I DON'T THINK
I'M HURT . . .

WE'RE ALL
RIGHT.

SOME OF THE GRAINS OF
DUST ARE JAGGED, LIKE
BITS OF GROUND GLASS.

THEY
SCRATCH
MY SKIN.
BUT—

I'M
OKAY.

I'M FINE.

THE AIR IS FILLED WITH WHITE DUST.

IT'S LIKE WE'RE TRAPPED IN A SNOW GLOBE.

WHAT ARE YOUR NAMES?

RHONDA.

C-CATHERINE. ≥SNIFF≥

GARY.

I'M LEE. I WORK HERE.

OKAY. LEE, RHONDA, CATHERINE, AND GARY . . .

I'M WITH THE NEW YORK CITY FIRE DEPARTMENT. I'M GOING TO GET YOU OUT OF THIS SAFELY.

I WANT EVERYONE TO PUT A PIECE OF CLOTHING IN FRONT OF YOUR MOUTH.

IT'S NOT GOOD TO BREATHE THIS DUST.

LEE GRABS SOME WATER AND PAPER TOWELS.

TAKE THESE.

THANK YOU!

WHAT **WAS** THAT?

ANOTHER PLANE?

NO . . .

I THINK THE TOP PART OF ONE OF THE BUILDINGS CAME DOWN.

THE OTHERS HOLD HANDS AS THEY WALK UP THE STREET—

—AWAY FROM THE OVERWHELMING DUST.

BUT DAD AND I STOP AND LOOK SOUTH.

I READ A BOOK ABOUT WORLD WAR II LAST YEAR.

I SAW PICTURES OF CITIES THAT WERE BOMBED AND BURNED TO THE GROUND.

THAT'S WHAT NEW YORK CITY REMINDS ME OF NOW—

IT'S GONE...

WHAT'S GONE?

ONE OF THE TOWERS...

IT WASN'T JUST THE TOP PART. THE ENTIRE BUILDING COLLAPSED.

BUT NOTHING LOOKS LIKE THE WRECKAGE OF A COLLAPSED HIGH-RISE TO ME.

WHERE ARE THE BIG CHUNKS OF CONCRETE? HUNKS OF GLASS FROM THE THOUSANDS OF WINDOWS?

WHERE IS IT?

THE BUILDING?

IT'S ALL AROUND US.

THE DUST!

THAT *WAS* THE TOWER!

EVERY HOUR SEEMS TO BRING A NEW HORROR.

"TOWER ONE HAS NOW COLLAPSED. BOTH TOWERS ARE GONE . . .

"A THIRD PLANE HAS CRASHED INTO THE PENTAGON . . ."

YET ANOTHER PLANE CRASHED IN A PENNSYLVANIA FIELD JUST A FEW MOMENTS AGO . . .

WE'RE WAITING FOR MORE INFORMATION . . .

OTHER FIREFIGHTERS MAKE IT BACK, ONE BY ONE.

THEY'RE COVERED IN DUST AND ASH.

SOME OF THEM ARE BLEEDING.

THEY PEEL OFF THEIR HEAVY EQUIPMENT, BUT THEIR BODIES STILL SEEM WEIGHED DOWN.

I HEARD THAT MARK . . .

AND GEORGIE? AND CHIEF?

THE GUYS JUST SHAKE THEIR HEADS—

—THEIR FRIENDS ARE GONE.

HOURS PASS.

"WE NOW KNOW THAT THE FOURTH PLANE WAS ALSO HIJACKED ..."

BY THE AFTERNOON, THERE'S ONLY ONE PERSON WE HAVEN'T HEARD ABOUT FOR SURE— UNCLE BENNY.

I SAW HIM RUN UP THE STAIRS IN TOWER ONE ...

YOU KNOW BENNY ...

HE WAS GOING TO GET TO THOSE BURNING FLOORS AND RESCUE AS MANY PEOPLE AS HE COULD.

I CAN SEE THE DOOM IN THE GUYS' EYES WHEN THEY TALK ABOUT UNCLE BENNY.

I DON'T WANT TO THINK ABOUT WHERE HE MIGHT BE . . .

IF HE'S HURT . . .

OR WORSE.

I JUST KEEP MY EYES GLUED TO THE DOOR . . .

AND WAIT.

About two months later.

Sunday, November 4, 2001

TWEEEEEE

LUCAS!

HEY, LUCAS!

HEY, JAMES!

TELLING THE TWINS APART IS EASY NOW.

GREAT GAME!

REALLY? COOL—HIGH FIVE!

WHACK

I KNEW THIS WOULD BE A TOUGH DAY.

I TAKE A MINUTE TO PULL MYSELF TOGETHER—

THE NIGHT OF THE FUNERAL, AS I GOT INTO BED, DAD STAYED BEHIND, LIKE HE USED TO.

I KNOW IT'S HARD RIGHT NOW, LUCAS.

IT WILL GET EASIER IN TIME.

HE DOESN'T MEAN "EASY."

HE MEANS THERE WILL BE MINUTES WHEN I'M NOT STUCK IN THE TERROR OF THAT SEPTEMBER DAY...

WHEN I'M NOT THINKING ABOUT THE PLANES OR THE PEOPLE WHO DIED IN THE TOWERS...

WHEN I'M NOT BURIED BY SADNESS.

THE STANDS ARE FULL OF LADDER 177 GUYS AND THEIR FAMILIES, CHEERING FOR MARK'S BOYS.

TWEEEET

GO JAMES! GO JASON!

HALF THE JAGUARS TEAM IS HERE TOO.

GO LUCAS!

I'M NOT ON THE TEAM ANYMORE...

BUT I HAVEN'T LOST FOOTBALL *OR* THE GUYS.

AND LAST WEEK, DAD BROUGHT THE SEAGRAVE MODEL UP FROM THE BASEMENT.

THE REAL RIG IS WRECKED, SO I FIGURED WE SHOULD FINISH THIS ONE.

MAYBE GIVE IT A PLACE OF HONOR IN THE FIREHOUSE?

YEAH!

WE WORK ON IT ON NIGHTS WHEN WE CAN'T SLEEP.

SOMETIMES MOM SITS WITH US.

NOW ALL WE'VE GOT LEFT ARE THE FINISHING TOUCHES.

THAT'S ONE GOOD THING THAT CAME OUT OF THAT DAY.

DAD AND I MARCHED OUT OF THE DUST...

AND WE JUST KEPT MARCHING ON.

TOGETHER.

TOUCHDOWN!

THE SCORE IS TIED IN THE FOURTH QUARTER.

THE OTHER TEAM CALLS A TIME-OUT.

OUR TEAM RUNS TO THE SIDELINES AND SURROUNDS OUR COACH—

UHHH . . .

UNCLE BENNY SAVED THAT MAN'S LIFE . . .

BUT HE WAS IN PRETTY BAD SHAPE HIMSELF.

WORD DIDN'T REACH THE FIREHOUSE UNTIL THAT EVENING.

THAT'S A MEMORY I'LL ALWAYS KEEP IN MY HEART . . .

THE MOMENT I KNEW UNCLE BENNY WAS SAFE.

TWEEEE

THE TIME-OUT IS OVER . . .

WE WAIT FOR THE SNAP

IT'S A TERRIBLE PASS . . .

IMPOSSIBLE TO CATCH . . .

JAMES GOES FOR IT ANYWAY.

THE CROWD CHEERS.

HEY, WATCH THAT KID GO . . .

HA-HA!

HE RUNS WITH ALL HIS MIGHT.

HE JUMPS . . .

FEARLESS . . .

. . . INTO THE BRIGHT BLUE SKY.

**TURN THE PAGE
TO READ MORE ABOUT
THE REAL-LIFE EVENTS OF**

SEPTEMBER 11, 2001

Dear Readers,

It was not part of my original plan to write about September 11, 2001, in the I Survived series. But I received more than a thousand emails from kids. "Will you be writing about 9/11?" they asked.

At first, my answer was always no. I was shocked that you would be so curious about that terrible day. I have friends who lost family members on 9/11 and others who narrowly escaped the towers before they collapsed. The memories of that day remain sharp and terrifying.

Though I work in New York City, in an office about a mile from the World Trade Center, I was not in NYC when the planes struck . . .

I WAS ON A PLANE ABOVE THE ATLANTIC OCEAN.

"WE HOPE YOU ARE ENJOYING YOUR FLIGHT. IT'S A WARM DAY IN NEW YORK CITY, WITH A HIGH OF EIGHTY-ONE DEGREES . . ."

I WAS HEADING BACK HOME AFTER A FAMILY REUNION AND CELEBRATION IN LONDON.

I HAD SAID GOODBYE TO MY HUSBAND, DAVID, IN LONDON.

HE WAS STAYING FOR THE WEDDING OF A BUSINESS FRIEND.

I COULDN'T WAIT TO SEE MY KIDS AND MY PARENTS, WHO WOULD BE WAITING FOR ME AT A LITTLE LEAGUE GAME IN OUR TOWN

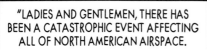

—ABOUT THIRTY-FIVE MILES FROM NEW YORK CITY.

AN HOUR AND A HALF INTO THE FLIGHT, I SUDDENLY HAD THE FEELING THAT THE PLANE WAS MAKING A SLOW TURN.

I HOPED I WAS IMAGINING IT BUT—

"LADIES AND GENTLEMEN, THERE HAS BEEN A CATASTROPHIC EVENT AFFECTING ALL OF NORTH AMERICAN AIRSPACE.

"WE ARE RETURNING TO LONDON. WE WILL PROVIDE MORE INFORMATION SHORTLY."

A CATASTROPHIC EVENT? WAS THERE AN EARTHQUAKE? A BOMB?

MAYBE A METEOR HIT THE UNITED STATES?

"LADIES AND GENTLEMEN . . ."

THREE PLANES WERE HIJACKED BY TERRORISTS AND FLOWN INTO THE WORLD TRADE CENTER AND THE PENTAGON.

THERE COULD BE OTHER PLANES INVOLVED . . . THE DISASTER IS STILL UNFOLDING.

WHEN WE LANDED IN LONDON, POLICE ESCORTED US INTO THE CHAOTIC AIRPORT.

I DIDN'T HAVE ANY MONEY, BUT A NICE TAXI DRIVER TOOK ME TO MY HUSBAND'S HOTEL.

WE BOTH CRIED THE WHOLE WAY.

DAVID AND I WEREN'T ABLE TO GET A CALL THROUGH TO OUR KIDS UNTIL LATE THAT NIGHT.

IT WAS FOUR MORE DAYS BEFORE PLANES BEGAN FLYING TO THE UNITED STATES AGAIN—

—AND WE COULD GET HOME TO OUR FAMILY.

I'D NEVER HUGGED THEM SO TIGHT.

The city slowly came back to life. Today, while the horrors of that day still linger, people have done their best to move forward.

So why did I write this book? Because after talking to many of you, I began to understand: 9/11 shaped the world you were born into. It's only natural that you would be curious about it. I hope my story gives you a sense of that day—the fear and the courage, the sense of horror and shock.

I will admit that in my plans for this story, Uncle Benny did not survive. I had it in my mind that he charged up the stairs of Tower One with fifty pounds of gear on his back. Lucas waited for him to return to the firehouse, but he never did.

But as I wrote the last page with Lucas on the football field, suddenly there was Uncle Benny. He just appeared. I could picture him so clearly, still banged up, but his eyes sparkling, looking at me as if to say, "Come on, there was so much sadness that day. Could you please give Lucas's story a happy ending?" And so I did.

Keep reading to learn more about 9/11 and the heroes who risked everything to help their fellow New Yorkers, with Lucas, Uncle Benny, Dad, and Mom to guide you.

TIMELINE

SEPTEMBER 11, 2001

8:46 A.M.	A commercial jet, **AMERICAN AIRLINES FLIGHT 11**, crashes into the North Tower (Tower One) of the World Trade Center.
9:03 A.M.	Another jet, **UNITED AIRLINES FLIGHT 175**, crashes into the South Tower (Tower Two) of the World Trade Center.
9:25 A.M.	United States airspace begins shutting down. No planes are allowed to take off.
9:37 A.M.	**AMERICAN AIRLINES FLIGHT 77** crashes into the Pentagon, the headquarters of the United States military, in Arlington County, Virginia.
9:59 A.M.	The **SOUTH TOWER** of the World Trade Center begins to collapse. People from around the country and the world watch it on TV.
10:03 A.M.	A fourth and final jet, **UNITED AIRLINES FLIGHT 93**, crashes into a field near Shanksville, Pennsylvania. It is later learned that Flight 93 was intended for either the United States Capitol building or the White House in Washington, DC. Passengers on that plane had learned of the crashes at the World Trade Center and the Pentagon. They stormed the cockpit and tried to regain control of the plane from the terrorists.
10:28 A.M.	The **NORTH TOWER** of the World Trade Center collapses.

WHEN THE BUILDINGS COLLAPSED, THE DUST REACHED THE EMPIRE STATE BUILDING, ALMOST THREE MILES AWAY.

THE FIRST RESPONDERS

IN THE MINUTES, HOURS, AND DAYS AFTER THE TOWERS COLLAPSED, THOUSANDS OF **FIREFIGHTERS AND OTHER RESCUE WORKERS** SWARMED THE SIXTEEN-ACRE DISASTER ZONE, SEARCHING FOR SURVIVORS.

MANY CAME BECAUSE THEY WERE CALLED BY THEIR DEPARTMENTS, BUT OTHER INDIVIDUALS SIMPLY SHOWED UP, HELPING HOWEVER THEY COULD.

THE AREA, WHICH BECAME KNOWN AS **GROUND ZERO**, WAS EXTREMELY DANGEROUS.

UNDERGROUND FIRES SMOLDERED, AND THE SMOKE WAS A **TOXIC** MIX OF MELTED PLASTIC, STEEL, LEAD, AND MANY OTHER POISONOUS CHEMICALS.

AFTER BREATHING IN THESE TOXINS, MANY FIRST RESPONDERS AND VOLUNTEERS BECAME SICK WITH **CANCER OR OTHER ILLNESSES**.

IN RESPONSE TO THIS, THE U.S. GOVERNMENT CREATED THE **SEPTEMBER 11ᵀᴴ VICTIMS COMPENSATION FUND**. IT HELPS THOSE WHO GOT SICK PAY THEIR MEDICAL BILLS. BUT MANY FAMILIES ARE STILL FEELING THE EFFECTS OF THAT DAY, EVEN TWENTY YEARS LATER.

IN THE FRIGHTENING AND UNCERTAIN DAYS AFTER 9/11, THE FIRST RESPONDERS AND OTHER VOLUNTEERS BROUGHT THE AMERICAN PEOPLE **HOPE**.

AFTER THE ATTACKS

A TEAM OF MEN ORGANIZED THE ATTACK. BUT THE MAN MOST RESPONSIBLE WAS **OSAMA BIN LADEN**. HE WAS THE LEADER OF A TERRORIST GROUP CALLED AL QAEDA (AL-**KYE**-DUH). THE GROUP'S HEADQUARTERS WAS IN THE COUNTRY OF AFGHANISTAN (AF-**GAN**-IH-STAN).

PRESIDENT GEORGE W. BUSH DEMANDED THAT AFGHANISTAN'S GOVERNMENT CAPTURE BIN LADEN AND HAND HIM OVER TO THE UNITED STATES. THE GOVERNMENT OF AFGHANISTAN, THEN CONTROLLED BY A GROUP CALLED THE TALIBAN, REFUSED.

ON OCTOBER 7, 2001, THE UNITED STATES, JOINED BY FORCES FROM OTHER COUNTRIES, DECLARED **WAR ON AFGHANISTAN**. THESE FORCES TOPPLED THE TALIBAN GOVERNMENT AND CAPTURED OR KILLED MANY MEMBERS OF AL QAEDA. BUT OSAMA BIN LADEN REMAINED ON THE RUN.

AFTER A TEN-YEAR MANHUNT, OSAMA BIN LADEN WAS DISCOVERED TO BE HIDING IN THE COUNTRY OF PAKISTAN. ON A TOP-SECRET MISSION ON MAY 2, 2011, BIN LADEN WAS KILLED BY MEMBERS OF A SPECIAL OPERATIONS UNIT OF THE UNITED STATES NAVY— **SEAL TEAM 6**.

"NAVY **SEALS**" IS A NICKNAME FOR THE U.S. NAVY **SEA**, **AIR**, AND **LAND** TEAMS. SEALS GO ON SECRET MISSIONS AROUND THE WORLD.

THE WAR IN AFGHANISTAN DRAGGED ON FOR MANY YEARS, COSTING THE LIVES OF APPROXIMATELY 16,000 AFGHANI PEOPLE AND 2,400 AMERICAN TROOPS. AS OF 2021, AFTER **TWENTY YEARS OF CONFLICT**, THERE ARE PLANS TO WITHDRAW AMERICAN TROOPS FROM AFGHANISTAN.

HONORING THOSE WE LOST

A TOTAL OF 2,977 PEOPLE DIED AS A RESULT OF THE 9/11 ATTACKS: 2,753 AT THE WORLD TRADE CENTER (OF WHICH 412 WERE NEW YORK CITY FIRST RESPONDERS); 184 PEOPLE AT THE PENTAGON; AND 40 PEOPLE WHEN THE FOURTH HIJACKED PLANE CRASHED IN SHANKSVILLE, PENNSYLVANIA.

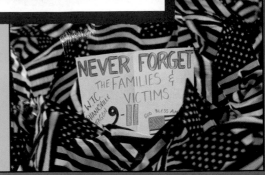

THE NATIONAL SEPTEMBER 11 MEMORIAL OPENED IN SEPTEMBER OF 2011. WHERE THE TWIN TOWERS ONCE STOOD, THERE ARE NOW TWO ENORMOUS REFLECTING POOLS SURROUNDED BY TWO OF THE LARGEST WATERFALLS IN NORTH AMERICA. THE NAMES OF ALL THE VICTIMS ARE CARVED INTO BRONZE PANELS CIRCLING THE MEMORIAL POOLS.

UNDERNEATH THE MEMORIAL IS THE NATIONAL 9/11 MEMORIAL MUSEUM, WHICH IS DEDICATED TO EXPLORING BOTH THE EVENTS OF 9/11 AND THE LASTING IMPACT.

EVERY YEAR ON SEPTEMBER 11, AN ART PIECE CALLED TRIBUTE IN LIGHT ILLUMINATES THE SKY IN REMEMBRANCE. IT IS MADE UP OF 88 SEARCHLIGHTS ARRANGED IN TWO GIANT SQUARES.

THE TOWERS OF LIGHT CAN BE SEEN FROM 60 MILES AWAY!

NEW YORK CITY, THEN AND NOW

WHEN THE **TWIN TOWERS** WERE COMPLETED IN 1973, THEY WERE THE TALLEST BUILDINGS IN THE MANHATTAN SKYLINE.

THE TOWER BUILT AFTER THE ATTACK, **ONE WORLD TRADE CENTER**, OPENED IN 2014.

MORE 9/11 BOOKS TO EXPLORE

Baskin, Nora Raleigh. *Nine, Ten: A September 11 Story.*
New York: Atheneum, 2016.

Gratz, Alan. *Ground Zero.* New York: Scholastic, 2021.

Rhodes, Jewel Parker. *Towers Falling.*
New York: Little, Brown, 2016.

SELECTED BIBLIOGRAPHY

Coe, Andrew. *FDNY: An Illustrated History of the Fire Department of New York City.* Hong Kong: Odyssey Books and Maps, 2003.

Dwyer, Jim, and Kevin Flynn. *102 Minutes: The Untold Story of the Fight to Survive Inside the Twin Towers.* New York: Henry Holt and Company, 2005.

Halberstam, David. *Firehouse.* New York: Hachette, 2002.

The National Commission on Terrorist Attacks Upon the United States. *The 9/11 Commission Report.* July 26, 2004.

Wright, Lawrence. *The Looming Tower.* New York: Knopf, 2006.

LAUREN TARSHIS'S

NEW YORK TIMES BESTSELLING I SURVIVED SERIES TELLS STORIES OF YOUNG PEOPLE AND THEIR RESILIENCE AND STRENGTH IN THE MIDST OF UNIMAGINABLE DISASTERS AND TIMES OF TURMOIL. LAUREN HAS BROUGHT HER SIGNATURE WARMTH, INTEGRITY, AND EXHAUSTIVE RESEARCH TO TOPICS SUCH AS THE BATTLE OF D-DAY, THE AMERICAN REVOLUTION, HURRICANE KATRINA, THE BOMBING OF PEARL HARBOR, AND OTHER WORLD EVENTS. LAUREN LIVES IN CONNECTICUT WITH HER FAMILY, AND CAN BE FOUND ONLINE AT LAURENTARSHIS.COM.

GEORGIA BALL

HAS WRITTEN COMICS FOR MANY OF HER FAVORITE CHILDHOOD CHARACTERS, INCLUDING STRAWBERRY SHORTCAKE, TRANSFORMERS, LITTLEST PET SHOP, MY LITTLE PONY, AND THE DISNEY PRINCESSES. IN ADDITION TO ADAPTING LAUREN TARSHIS'S I SURVIVED SERIES TO GRAPHIC NOVELS, GEORGIA WRITES ABOUT HISTORICAL EVENTS SUCH AS THE WORLD WAR II BATTLES OF KURSK AND GUADALCANAL. GEORGIA LIVES WITH HER HUSBAND, DAUGHTER, AND RAMBUNCTIOUS PETS IN FLORIDA. VISIT HER ONLINE AT GEORGIABALLAUTHOR.COM.

COREY EGBERT

LOVES ILLUSTRATING STORIES THAT EMPOWER AND INSPIRE YOUNG PEOPLE. THIS IS HIS FIRST GRAPHIC NOVEL. HE LIVES WITH HIS WIFE, SON, AND TWO CATS IN A LITTLE HOUSE BY THE WOODS IN VIRGINIA. YOU CAN SEE MORE OF HIS WORK AT COREYEGBERT.COM.

CHI NGO

IS A VIETNAMESE ILLUSTRATOR/ANIMATION ARTIST LOCATED IN LOS ANGELES. SHE HAS CONTRIBUTED TO BRANDS LIKE TRANSFORMERS AND CLIFFORD AND WORKED FOR CARTOON NETWORK, NETFLIX, HASBRO, AND BENTOBOX. YOU CAN SEE MORE OF HER WORK AT CHI-NGO.COM.